driftwood

sponges

wishing
stone

sea glass

heart-shaped
stones

skipping stones

author's note

The author gratefully acknowledges the love, support, and contributions of the following people,
without whom the development of this book would not have been possible:
Rhona and Jerry Bass, Sondra and Allan Hochman, Celene Bass, Miles Bass, Rena LaFrance, Elizabeth Clift,
Anna Altmann, Lisa Pearce, Anna Johnson of AJ & Associates, Brandy Polay of Type B Design,
Miranda Hersey Helin of Pen and Press, and Donovan Bergman of Friesens.
Indirectly but serendipitously: Michael Park of Greenfield Books,
Burton Lysecki of Burton Lysecki Books, and Gregory Gillert from Justin G. Schiller Ltd., without whom
I would never have come to buy a painting, and perhaps never have written this book.
Lastly, thank you to my husband David Hochman, for everything.

Thank you to Lev Hochman who gave me the title and to Bette Woodland, for bringing this book to life.

Text copyright © 2012 by Marisa Hochman
Illustrations copyright © 2012 by Bette Woodland

Library and Archives Canada Cataloguing in Publication
Hochman, Marisa, 1976-
A walk in Pirate's Cove / written by Marisa Hochman ; illustrations
by Bette Woodland.
ISBN 978-0-9865679-0-2
1. Children's poetry, Canadian (English) I. Woodland, Bette II. Title.
PS8615.O24W35 2012   jC811'.6   C2011-907004-9

First edition 2012
10 9 8 7 6 5 4 3 2 1

Printed and bound in Canada by Friesens
This book was typeset in Baskerville
The illustrations were painted in oil paint on Multimedia Artboard
Book design by Brandy Polay of Type B Design
Copyediting by Miranda Hersey Helin of Pen and Press

Thirty Six Peonies Publishing Inc.
Winnipeg, Manitoba, Canada
Visit us at www.thirtysixpeonies.com

A Walk in Pirate's Cove

For Lev, Nathan, and Naomi and for my
husband David, with love and memories
of Pirate's Cove.
—M.H.

For my parents
Betty and Harry French, with love.
—B.W.

A Walk in Pirate's Cove

Written by
MARISA HOCHMAN

Illustrations by BETTE WOODLAND

36 PEONIES
PUBLISHING, INCORPORATED

WWW.THIRTYSIXPEONIES.COM

*L*et's go off on a pirate walk,

Down by the shining sea,

We'll take some paper bags with us,

In search of treasures three:

Bright sea glass, round black stones,

A few pink pearly shells,

Washed ashore by moonlit waves,

In rolling dips and swells.

On our way, we'll cross a bridge,

That spans a creek so wide,

Then dance our way across green fields,

Down to the waterside.

We'll dip our toes into the sand,

Pound shells to silken powder,

Throw stones,

kerplunk,

into the waves

To see whose splash is louder.

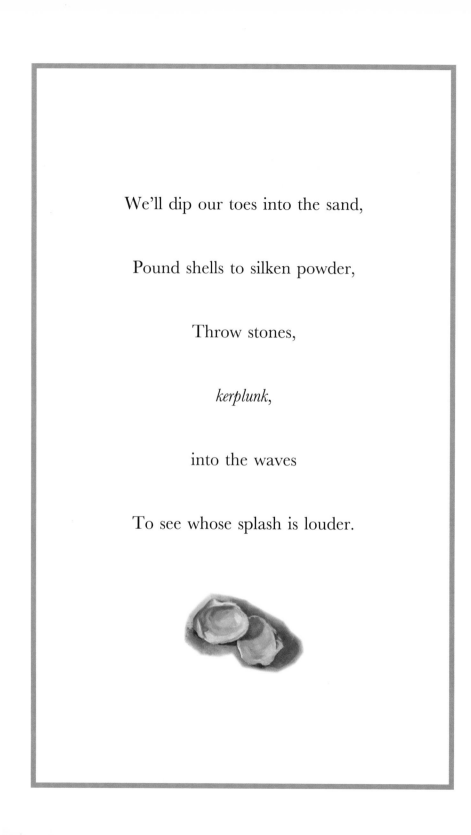

We'll make our way among the rocks,

Through scrub along the shore,

Filling our sacks with feathers and shells,

And pirate loot galore!

Scarce wishing stones and skipping stones,

Into our sacks will fall,

Alien stones with secret codes,

Smooth pebbles, large and small.

Then walking high on weathered wood,

Along the pier we'll go,

To gaze upon the sparkling waves

Of Pirate's Cove below.

Let's go stand on the

old marsh bridge,

To hear the blackbirds trill,

Watch dragonflies

with shimmering wings,

Skim the water still.

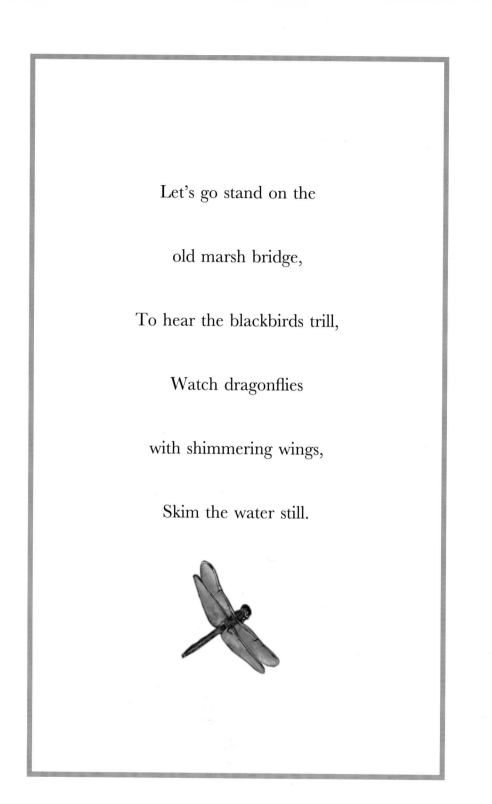

We'll drop some little pebbles down

To make soft rippling rings,

And listen to the marsh frogs croak

Their evening wonderings.

We'll gaze out past the rushes,

At gold trees far away,

And dream the world goes on like this,

Forever and a day.

Let's sleep out in the tent tonight,

Beneath a starry sky,

We'll roast marshmallows by firelight,

We'll walk to the pier in the pale moonlight,

To hear the waves roll by.

To hear the waves roll by...

To hear the waves roll by...

We'll sit on the pier

in the full moonlight,

To hear the waves roll by.

smooth white stones

alien stones

dragon's teeth

round black stones

pink heelsplitter mussel

pelican feather